THE
SPOOKY TAIL
OF
PREWITT PEACOCK

BILL PEET

HOUGHTON MIFFLIN COMPANY BOSTON

A TIGER FOR T. J.

ISBN 0-395-15494-4 REINFORCED EDITION

ISBN 0-395-28159-8 SANDPIPER EDITION

PRINTED IN THE UNITED STATES OF AMERICA

WOZ   20   19   18

Prewitt was a wild peacock who lived far out in the jungle where most wild peacocks live. However, Prewitt was not as proud as a peacock, for he had nothing at all to be proud of.

A peacock's great pride is in his glorious tail with all the beautiful blue-green eyespots. Prewitt's tail was no more than a few scraggly feathers with only two eyespots. His was indeed a sad tail. And Prewitt was indeed a sad peacock.

Phineas was the proudest of the peacocks, but then he had the most fanciful tail with many more beautiful eyespots than the others. So he was naturally the leader of the flock. Wherever they went Phineas always strutted proudly at the head of the procession with his tail fanned out in full glory.

Last, and by far the least, came Prewitt with his scraggly tail dragging behind him. But when it came to facing a tiger the other peacocks were not one bit better than Prewitt. They were all equally scared!

Fortunately, the peacocks had but one tiger to worry about. That was Travis, a scrawny, toothless old fellow. Other tigers had better things to do than chase peacocks and end up with a mouth full of feathers. But toothless old Travis could no longer afford to be choosy. He was down to such small game as toads and tadpoles. To him a peacock would be a fancy feast if he could ever catch one.

For such an old cat he was pretty spry and ever so sly. So the peacocks always kept an eye cocked for old Travis. The second he made his leap they took off like a shot, to go fluttering into a treetop. It was always a close call.

Once the peacocks had recovered from their fright, the first thing
they did was check their tails for fear they might have lost a feather.
Losing a tail feather was always heartbreaking for a peacock.

Prewitt's scraggly nothing of a tail was something he would never
need to worry about. At least so he thought. But then Prewitt was
in for a surprise!

His tail had more growing to do. Much more. One day he noticed that the eyespots had doubled in size, and fierce black eyebrows had sprouted just above them. And yet that was not the end of the tail. It continued to feather out. Before long a jagged mouth appeared just below the enormous eyes. Then finally out sprang a pair of feathery arms with wildly clutching claws.

"My tail has gone wild!" exclaimed Prewitt. "It's turned into a green-eyed monster! What a terrible tail! But then, after all," he sighed, "I grew it, so I suppose I'll just have to get used to it. I only hope the other peacocks can too."

The other peacocks paid so little attention to Prewitt that a week had passed before they discovered his tail had gone wild.
When they did it hit them all at once.

They let go with such terrified shrieks they could be heard all the way to Mandalay. It took ten minutes for Phineas to settle them down. Then in a fury he turned to Prewitt.

"What's come over you, Prewitt! What on earth have you done to your tail!" he squawked.

"Nothing," said Prewitt. "It just grew this way."

"The thing is downright spooky," said Phineas. "It gives me the creeps."

"It gives *me* the creeps too," said Prewitt, "but what can I do?"

"Keep it to yourself," said Phineas. "Hold it down! Living out here in the jungle is scary enough without that spooky tail of yours popping up."

Keeping his tail down was no problem for Prewitt. Since he was not the least bit proud, letting his tail drag the ground had been a longtime habit. But this was an entirely different tail, and not one bit droopy. It was springy. One afternoon, to Prewitt's surprise, up it sprang! And there was Phineas! And Phineas was furious!

"Prewitt!" he shrieked. "What did I tell you?"

"But-but," stammered Prewitt, "it's nothing but a bunch of feathers. Feathers can't hurt anyone."

"Feathers or not," said Phineas, "it scares the wits out of us. So you either get rid of the thing or leave the flock. Take your choice and let me know first thing in the morning."

When Prewitt settled down to roost for the night in a treetop his head was in a whirl.

"As awful as it is," he thought, "my new tail is better than no tail at all. Yet, if I keep it I must leave the flock and go wandering off all alone. Either way would be sad. So I'd better sleep on it, then decide in the morning."

As Prewitt slept he dreamed a weird dream. Out of a swirling mist came a teary-eyed elephant with no trunk. Then a sad, long-faced giraffe with no neck, followed by a sheepish-looking camel with no humps. And finally a pitiful peacock with no tail. It was Prewitt! And close behind were other peacocks all laughing at him. As the laughter exploded into wild cackling, the tailless peacock suddenly turned into a lizard and slithered under a rock.

The next morning Prewitt awakened in a cold sweat. After checking his tail feathers to make sure they were all there, he fluttered down to the ground to join the flock.

"Well," said Phineas, "have you decided? Do you go, or does your tail go?"

"We're both staying," said Prewitt. "So there!"

"Oh no you don't!" cried Phineas, "Come on everyone! Grab a feather! Off with his tail!"

As the peacocks closed in with beaks snapping Prewitt whirled about and took off through the jungle. The chase was on!

The peacocks were very poor flyers, so it was more of a fluttering, hopping, running chase. And although Prewitt was a bit smaller, with shorter legs, he was a bit quicker. By zigzagging in and out through the trees and darting under bushes and ferns Prewitt managed to dodge his pursuers. But try as he might he couldn't shake them. The peacocks kept right on his tail. Finally, in desperation he headed for an open field.

Prewitt figured they wouldn't dare follow. It was much too great a risk for a peacock to venture into the open. But dare they did! The peacocks were determined to catch Prewitt no matter what. And as he went plowing through the tall grass they were just a few steps behind, and gaining fast. Prewitt was just about to be caught when all of a sudden —!

A tiger reared up out of the grass! It was old Travis! And just like that the chase was over. It was too late to turn back, and with

no trees to flutter into the peacocks were doomed. They were too terrified to move, so they just stood there waiting for the finish. Then just as the tiger was all set to spring —!

— he let out a *YOWL* of terror. Then in a panic old Travis went leaping and bounding away to disappear in the distance. The peacocks were left stunned and bewildered.

"What could ever frighten a tiger?" they wondered as they looked

frantically about. Then all at once there it was. Prewitt's spooky tail! When Prewitt caught sight of the tiger the tail sprang straight up in all its horror. There was no doubt but what Prewitt's tail had saved the day.

When Phineas finally found his voice he cried, "Prewitt! Prewitt! How can we ever repay you?"

"There's no need to," said Prewitt. "It was nothing I did. It was my tail."

"Just the same," said Phineas, "you deserve a reward. How would you like to take my place? We would be proud to have you as our leader."

"Yes! Yes!" cried all the others. "Ever so proud!"

"Oh no," said Prewitt, "I'm not bossy enough to be the leader. Besides, I'd rather wander about just as I please."

"Then would you mind if we tag along?" asked Phineas. "Just to keep you company?"

"I don't mind at all," said Prewitt, "tag along if you like."

From that day on, wherever Prewitt went the other peacocks followed close behind. Very close. And with so many faithful followers Prewitt finally agreed to be their leader. They were behind him 100 percent. Of course Prewitt knew why, but just the same he couldn't help being proud.

Now at last Prewitt was truly as proud as a peacock.